A Dip

Written by Fiona Tomlinson

Illustrated by Ángeles Peinador

Collins

Tim pats it.

Tim dips in.

Tim sits in.

5

Dad pats it.

Dad dips in.

Dad sits in.

Nan pats it.

Nan dips in it.

Nan sits in it.

After reading

Letters and Sounds: Phase 2

Word count: 38

Focus phonemes: /s/ /a/ /t/ /p/ /i/ /n/ /m/ /d/

Curriculum links: Understanding the World

Early learning goals: Reading: read and understand simple sentences; use phonic knowledge to decode regular words and read them aloud accurately

Developing fluency

- Your child may enjoy hearing you read the book.
- Take turns to read a page and encourage your child to read the labels.

Phonic practice

- Turn to pages 2 and 3. Ask your child to find the words that contain the /t/ sound, and to blend, then read the words to check their own answers. (p/a/t/s – **pats**; i/t – **it**; T/i/m – **Tim**)
- Turn to pages 6 and 7. Ask your child to find the words that contain the /d/ sound. (D/a/d – **Dad**; d/i/p/s – **dips**)
- Turn to page 12. Ask your child to find and blend the two words with the /n/ sound. (N/a/n – **Nan**; i/n – **in**)
- Look at the "I spy sounds" pages (14 and 15). Ask your child if they can see something on the beach beginning with the /d/ sound (e.g. *doll, dress, dominoes*). Ask your child to find other things that begin with the /d/ sound anywhere in the picture (e.g. *dinosaur, Dad, dog, duck, drink, donuts*)

Extending vocabulary

- Look together at pages 10 and 11. Ask your child to explain who **pats** and **dips**. Can they mime doing each action to clarify the difference?
- Ask your child to read the sentence on page 11 and ask: What does Nan dip in? (e.g. *her fingertips*)